HERO OF THE MONTH!

A Random House PICTUREBACK® Book
Random House 🏠 New York

All Rights Reserved. Published in the United States by Random House Children's Books, a division of
Penguin Random House LLC, 1745 Broadway, New York, NY 10019, and in Canada by Penguin Random
House Canada Limited, Toronto. Pictureback, Random House, and the Random House colophon are
registered trademarks of Penguin Random House LLC.
randomhousekids.com
dcsuperherogirls.com
dckids.com
ISBN 978-1-5247-6604-7 (trade) — ISBN 978-1-5247-6605-4 (ebook)
MANUFACTURED IN CHINA
10 9 8 7 6 5 4 3 2 1
Lenticular cover effect and production: Red Bird Publishing Ltd., U.K.

AT SUPER HERO HIGH SCHOOL, the world's—and out-of-this-world's— mightiest teens train to be the heroes of tomorrow. Everyone has the potential to be a hero, and the students at Super Hero High make that goal a part of their everyday schedule, whether it's helping a fellow student ace a test or stopping a cosmic creature from crushing downtown Metropolis. When students really excel, they get recognized with the *HERO OF THE MONTH* award.

Here are just a few outstanding winners. . . .

★ POISON IVY ★

Poison Ivy is a bit on the shy side—in fact, she's more comfortable with plants than with people—but she's finally starting to blossom. Ever since a lab accident gave her incredible abilities with the plant kingdom, she's been quietly searching for ways to increase her superpowers so she can grow from a small acorn into a mighty oak!

Place of Origin:	Gotham City
Powers and Skills:	Ability to control plants and accelerate plant growth, biology genius
Specialty:	Green thumb

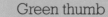

HERO OF THE MONTH

From overgrown (and hungry!) snapdragons to spine-slinging cacti, when plant life gets wilder and weedier than usual, Poison Ivy puts a stop to it!

BUMBLEBEE

Bumblebee is the ultimate fly on the wall! She's an upbeat engineering genius, and the high-tech suit she built allows her to fly, shrink, and blast shocking bee stings! Her shrinking skills get her into places no other Super can access. Beyond her save-the-day savvy, she also brings the best beats and cape-shaking music as the class DJ.

Place of Origin:	Metropolis
Powers and Skills:	Ability to shrink to the size of a bee, flight, super-strength in shrunken form
Weapon:	Blasters that emit electric stings
Specialties:	Extreme stealth, pulling off the best surprise parties

HERO OF THE MONTH

Consistently there to save the day, Bumblebee proves that great heroes can come in small packages!

SUPERGIRL

Supergirl is a new student from the planet Krypton. She's the most powerful teen at Super Hero High and on Earth! She might be a little clumsy while she learns to control all her amazing powers, but she never gives up.

Place of Origin:	The planet Krypton
Powers and Skills:	Super-strength, super-speed, flight, invulnerability, super-cold breath; special vision: X-ray, telescopic, microscopic, heat
Specialties:	Saving the day, being a super friend

HERO OF THE MONTH

Supergirl led the charge against Granny Goodness and her army of Furies and parademons when they tried to take over the school—and the world!

BATGIRL

Batgirl is an off-the-charts, just-forget-about-the-test super genius. Her greatest power is her brainpower! As a student, Batgirl is completely confident, cool, and collected. When she's not honing her detective skills, she's inventing high-tech gadgets, upgrading her Bat-Bunker, and making communication bracelets for all her friends.

Place of Origin:	Gotham City
Powers and Skills:	Advanced deduction and crime-fighting, computer and technological genius, martial arts
Specialties:	Keeping her cool in any situation, making mods to her Batjet, and updating her tech

HERO OF THE MONTH

Batgirl's bravery and tech savvy were instrumental in helping Supergirl stop the Furies.

WONDER WOMAN

Wonder Woman grew up on the island of Themyscira, which was populated with female warriors. As Princess of Themyscira, she's a natural-born leader, and it's her mission to make the entire universe a better place. She chose to attend Super Hero High with the goal of becoming the greatest hero she can be!

Place of Origin:	Themyscira
Powers and Skills:	Super-strength, super-speed, flight
Weapons:	The magic Lasso of Truth, indestructible bracelets, and a shield of Themysciran steel
Specialties:	Deflecting lasers, bullets, and projectiles of all types with her unbreakable bracelets

HERO OF THE MONTH

She has stopped skyscraper-tall Giganta and faced villains as powerful as her own uncle Ares, the ancient god of war. But Wonder Woman's ability to befriend anyone and be a strong, inspirational leader are what won her the Hero of the Month award.

KATANA

Katana wields her sword with skill, style, and grace! She has traveled around the world and is always on the cutting edge of fashion. She's fearless and uber funky. When she's not fighting crime, Katana is sharpening her skills as a designer and an artist.

Place of Origin:	Japan
Powers and Skills:	Martial arts, sword fighting, and the ability to make a weapon out of just about anything
Weapons:	Sword, throwing stars
Specialty:	Fighting crime with style!

HERO OF THE MONTH

Always a cut above the rest, Katana has the steel to take on any challenge. She's noble and always ready to help the helpless, and she does so with fierce fashion and amazing style.

These are just a few of Super Hero High's standout students. Who will be the next *HERO OF THE MONTH*: Cheetah? Starfire? Arrowette? *YOU?*

Always remember that good deeds, kindness, and friendly gestures—big or small—can make someone else's day *SUPER*.